The Diary of Grace Darling
By Sarah Lee

This work is fiction based on the life of Grace Darling.

The Diary of Grace Darling© 2014 by Sarah Lee

All rights reserved. No part of this publication may be reproduced, distributed, or transmitted in any form or by any means, including photocopying, recording, or other electronic or mechanical methods, without the prior written permission of the publisher, except in the case of brief quotations embodied in critical reviews and certain other non-commercial uses permitted by copyright law.

24th November 1825

My name is Grace Horsley Darling. It's my birthday! I am ten years old today. My father says I'm almost a young woman. I am so happy I have been given this beautiful diary, I am so lucky. I can now record my life story. I hope I have an exciting life story to tell, but as I am only ten years old I still have to experience lots of things. I have always wanted a diary, and I am so thankful my dear father and mother have bought me this beautiful leather diary. My sister Mary bought me a new quill and ink well so that I write beautifully, and my brother William made me a box to keep my shells in, and Job gave me a book, 'Robinson Crusoe' I am so lucky, I am so looking forward to reading it. I got lots of other presents too. My beautiful sister Thomasin must have worked so hard, and in secret to make me a beautiful pink dress, I shall wear it to my party tonight, it will be so much fun. My father said I need to have a lovely fun day today, after what happened last week; I had another nightmare about that last night, and I can't seem to shake the memory of it off.

I had been sleeping soundly when I was awoken by the sensation of icy cold water on my back. The force of the water pushed me from my bed and before I knew what was happening the water was almost to the ceiling of my bedroom. I was able to keep afloat by kicking my legs, my head was just inches from the ceiling, and I feared if any more water came in I would sure be drowned. I prayed to God to save me, and I screamed Help! From the top of my lungs. I was trying to keep my wits about me, and tried not to panic; I looked around to see if I could see a way out.

The window was very small it was open but too small for me to get through but I tried to break the bigger pain of glass under the smaller window. I kicked it with my bare feet to try and crack the glass but it held strong. The moonlight revealed the top of the door frame and I knew the door was shut, and was unsure whether I could pull the door open against the heaviness of the water that had now filled my room. The air was scant, as I only had a few inches between the top of the water and the ceiling from which to breathe. I looked around to see if I could use something to break the window. The water was coming in through a gap above the window sill and through the open window. My dolls and some books were floating on top of the water. Just as I was about to go and have another try at kicking the window my brother Job's face popped up out of the water. He was such a welcoming sight, but he too looked worried. 'You need to swim to the doorway, then swim under the water and under the doorframe.' He knew I wasn't a very good swimmer. 'I'll be here don't worry; just don't take a breath till your head is up out of the water.'

    I did as he said and swam to the door frame, but the door frame was disappearing under the water. I aimed for the direction where I had remembered it, and felt the wall with my hands, and then felt the doorframe. I kept my hand on the doorframe and dove beneath the water, and within seconds found myself at the stairs, I was almost at the top of the stairs. I grabbed the banister and pulled myself onto the stair not covered with water and sat for a while panting. Job soon joined me. My family were all stood at the top of the stairs. They shouted for me to go to them and they hugged me so tight. My mother was crying. Job got a big hug from father for his bravery. We were all safe thank God. There had been a fierce storm, and the surge of the waves had toppled over our Island and flooded the downstairs completely. Luckily the animals outside were on higher ground and were safe although my dear eider duck Cussy would have enjoyed the weather. My room is downstairs. Father said I would never have to sleep downstairs again, and they would have to make room for me in Thomasin's and Mary's room. Our house is very crowded, although my brother William now nineteen is living in Alnwick working as a joiner, there are still many living here. Mother and Father, my twin sisters Thomasin and Mary Ann who are seventeen, brother Job now fifteen, sister Elizabeth Grace, Betsy, who is thirteen, my brother Robert who is eleven, and my younger twin brothers, George and William Brookes, who are now just six years old, so you see ten in total, a lot to squeeze in this tiny cottage on Brownsman Island. The lighthouse tower is next to the cottage but there is no room in there for any people to sleep. I hope Thomasin and Mary don't snore like father does.

    I better get ready for the party I will write again tomorrow.

25th November 1825

We had such a good time last night. We had a scrumptious meal of roast duck and orange sauce. But I enjoyed the tartlets and iced pudding the best. Father played his fiddle and we sang songs, danced and played some fun games. Brooks ate too much and went to bed with a sore tummy, and father was a little dizzy after drinking his ale and he nearly fell into the hearth, but it was fun everyone was so happy. It is sad though that we have to leave this house. I love it here. Father has been told he needs to be the Lighthouse keeper of the new lighthouse they are building on Longstone Island. It is about a mile further out to sea. It is a barren land, only rock, and no grass, nowhere to play or breed our animals. Father said the sheep and rabbits will have to stay on Brownsman Island, but my little friend Fluffy rabbit, and my Cussy will miss me, and I will miss them, so I cannot go without them. Father said I can still visit Brownsman Island, he said he will row me here whenever he has time off. Father is still going to grow crops here, so they will need tending to, and the animals too need looking after, so I may get to come here quite often, and father is going to teach me how to row too.

I love it here on Brownsman Island it is glorious in the summer. We are so lucky to have our own island. We can see for miles. Bamburgh Castle is so grand and such a wonderful view in the morning sun and when the sun sets behind the castle, it is so beautiful. We never have to worry about disturbing the neighbours with the noise we make, as our neighbours are the seabirds, and seals, and they make more noise than we do at times. Living so close to these creatures and watching how they communicate with each other, and watching them grow, is such a rare treat to behold, we feel like we are part of nature, in touch with God's creation. None of us want to leave here, even father. He says the new lighthouse is bigger and more modern than the one he keeps now, but what is worrying is that all of the rooms are inside the lighthouse tower. I think they must be very small rooms, because I can see the tower from here and it looks very narrow, although it is far away; I cannot imagine how they have managed to build rooms inside. Father said there are five rooms inside. I am afraid we will be all squashed like rabbits in burrows. But we will also be further away from the mainland, and even now it takes hours to row to shore, so if we are even further away it will be harder to go and visit my cousins in Bamburgh, or go to the theatre, or go to the shops. Father said I should not worry my pretty little head over it and let him do the worrying, but I can't help it. We still have a few months left here before we need to move and I have been told to sort out my belongings as I can't take everything with me, he said there is not enough storage space. It will be hard to decide what to leave behind; I love all of my things. Especially my dear Fluffy and Cussy. I must go and play with them now, I can't bear to think of leaving them here.

25th December 1825

Happy Christmas! I love Christmas it's my favourite time of the year. We have been so busy today. I helped mother with the cooking, we had roast goose, and I made the plum pudding. Father said it was the best plum pudding he had ever tasted. We were visited by my aunts and uncles and my cousins came and shared in the fun. We had to have our meals on our laps as there wasn't enough room around the table, but we didn't mind. Santa Claus had been so kind to us. I was given some new dolls, as my other ones were damaged in the flood I wonder how he knew about that. I was also given some new books, some clothes, and some games.

My brothers and sisters were very happy with their presents and loved what I had made for them. I am so glad Thomasin had taught me how to knit, they are so grateful for the gloves I had made them, it gets very cold here in the winter. My father loves the hat I knitted, it fits him a treat, and my mother loves her scarf. I have spent so much time knitting I have had so little time to do any writing.

Father gives me writing tasks though. My brothers go to the school in the castle, but father teaches us girls at home. However I have been so lucky his time has been spent rowing backwards and forwards to the new lighthouse that I have had more time to make their gifts. I am writing this by candle light, whilst my sisters are sleeping, I just had to write it down else it would be forgotten.

Father read a poem from my new book 'A Visit from St Nicholas.'

A Visit from St. Nicholas

'Twas the night before Christmas, when all through the house

Not a creature was stirring, not even a mouse;

The stockings were hung by the chimney with care,

In hopes that St. Nicholas soon would be there;

The children were nestled all snug in their beds;

While visions of sugar-plums danced in their heads;

And mamma in her 'kerchief, and I in my cap,

Had just settled our brains for a long winter's nap,

When out on the lawn there arose such a clatter,

I sprang from my bed to see what was the matter.

Away to the window I flew like a flash,

Tore open the shutters and threw up the sash.

The moon on the breast of the new-fallen snow,

Gave a lustre of midday to objects below,

When what to my wondering eyes did appear,

But a miniature sleigh and eight tiny rein-deer,

With a little old driver so lively and quick,

I knew in a moment he must be St. Nick.

More rapid than eagles his coursers they came,

And he whistled, and shouted, and called them by name:

"Now, *Dasher*! now, *Dancer*! now *Prancer* and *Vixen*!

On, *Comet*! on, *Cupid*! on, *Donder* and *Blixen*!

To the top of the porch! to the top of the wall!

Now dash away! dash away! dash away all!"

As leaves that before the wild hurricane fly,

When they meet with an obstacle, mount to the sky;

So up to the housetop the coursers they flew

With the sleigh full of toys, and St. Nicholas too——

And then, in a twinkling, I heard on the roof

The prancing and pawing of each little hoof.

As I drew in my head, and was turning around,

Down the chimney St. Nicholas came with a bound.

He was dressed all in fur, from his head to his foot,

And his clothes were all tarnished with ashes and soot;

A bundle of toys he had flung on his back,

And he looked like a pedler just opening his pack.

His eyes—how they twinkled! his dimples, how merry!

His cheeks were like roses, his nose like a cherry!

His droll little mouth was drawn up like a bow,

And the beard on his chin was as white as the snow;

The stump of a pipe he held tight in his teeth,

And the smoke, it encircled his head like a wreath;

He had a broad face and a little round belly

That shook when he laughed, like a bowl full of jelly.

He was chubby and plump, a right jolly old elf,

And I laughed when I saw him, in spite of myself;

A wink of his eye and a twist of his head

Soon gave me to know I had nothing to dread;

He spoke not a word, but went straight to his work,

And filled all the stockings; then turned with a jerk,

And laying his finger aside of his nose,

And giving a nod, up the chimney he rose;

He sprang to his sleigh, to his team gave a whistle,

And away they all flew like the down of a thistle.

But I heard him exclaim, ere he drove out of sight—

'Happy Christmas to all, and to all a good night!'

We too had hung our stockings on the mantle. I had looked outside on Christmas Eve around midnight, in the hope of catching sight of Santa Claus and his reindeers, but could only see the stars and the moon. I did though wonder at one point if I heard the jingle of bells, but it may have just been the whisper of the surf hitting the rocks, I will never know. Unfortunately I fell asleep soon after and was woken by my sister Mary shouting 'It's Christmas! Wake up! Let us go downstairs and see if Santa has been.' It has been such an exciting day, but I am so sleepy now I fear I could sleep for a week.

February 16th 1826

It was a sad day when we left our home. We all wandered around the empty rooms remembering what happy times we had had. I cried when I had to say goodbye to Fluffy and Cussy. I can see our house from my new bedroom, it looks so far away. It took a long time for father to row us here, over an hour. The first thing I noticed about our new home was the lighthouse. It is enormous, stretching up to the sky. The rocky Island we now live on is very bare. When we arrived we were greeted by a young seal pup, he flapped his flippers when he saw us as if he was pleased to see us. He is so cute, with beautiful big eyes, a cute nose and long whiskers. His fur is a sandy colour. I went to stroke him but as I got near to him he crawled towards the edge of the rocks and flopped into the ocean. I hope he comes back.

Next to the lighthouse is a small stone building with a wooden door. 'What's that Father?' I asked.

'It's the barracks, they built it for the workmen when they had to stay over to shelter them from the wind and rain, but the roof is damaged, so it's not used for anything now, it's not even suitable to store anything inside, the roof needs to be fixed first.'

Father showed us around inside the lighthouse, the ground floor is the living room. It is smaller than our other house and it is a complete circle. The furniture in the room has been very cleverly designed to fit the curved walls. We followed father upstairs to the next room. It was to be the boys room, all of the boys will have to sleep here. That's Job, Robert, George and Brookes, yet there are only two beds, one on top of the other encased in a wooden frame.

The boys all looked depressed when they saw the room. 'I will be leaving soon anyway,' said Job. 'Me too!' said Robert. 'I want the top bunk,' shouted George.

The next floor up was Mother and Father's room. It did not look very homely. Mother tried to look cheerful. 'We have a lovely view, look!' It was true the views were lovely, we could see for miles. 'Come on girls I'll show you your room.' We followed father up the stairs to our room. Thomasin, Betsy, Mary and I looked at each other. Mary began to cry. 'I want to go home,' she sobbed. Mother comforted her, hugging her tight. It was identical to the boy's room. 'You will have to share a bed for now, there is not enough space to put in another two beds unfortunately,' said Father in a matter of fact tone of voice. 'You will just have to sleep head to toe for the time being. '

'I shall leave then,' said Thomasin. 'I shall go and live with our Cousins in Bamburgh.' Father didn't say anything. I was hoping he would tell her not to be silly, but he seemed to accept her offer of leaving. 'Father I don't want anybody to leave, this place is so bare, it will be truly dreadful if they leave, really horrid.' I too began crying. I knew Father wanted us to be happy; he had been given a wage rise for moving to the new lighthouse, from fifty pounds a year to seventy pounds a year. 'I am sorry kids, there is nothing I can do, Trinity have decided they want to decommission the other lighthouse and next week it will light no more. I am powerless to do anything about it. We need to trust God, he has brought us here, our job is to protect the sailors, this light will warn them of these dangerous rocks, many have already lost their lives here crashing into the rocks, this lighthouse will shine for miles out to sea, warning the ships not to stray near here, we are here to do God's work, to warn the sailors.'

Father made sense. It was an important job being the Lighthouse keeper. Someone needed to make sure the light was lit and in working order, and they needed to live here as it was a twenty four hour job. I was being selfish thinking of myself, we needed to think of the poor sailors whose lives we must protect. I dried my tears and went over to Father and squeezed his hand. He smiled a warm smile at me and he hugged me, then the others joined and we had one big family group hug. Father made me proud to be alive, to help do God's work, we were privileged to be chosen to have such responsibility, after all I doubt God would give this job to just anyone, my Father, our family were here for a reason.

Father then led us to the top floor, it was to be our storage area and was already filled with our belongings all still in boxes. I ran to my box and pulled out my favourite doll Flo, and hugged her tight, then followed the others up the steep ladder to the light. It was much bigger than our other lighthouse lamp; the tower on Brownsman Island had a coal fire as the light. Father needed to climb a ladder on the outside of the tower to light it and keep it burning. This new lamp was dazzling. It had a small lamp in the centre; the wick was unlit and was surrounded by huge prisms of glass that were arranged like spokes on a wheel. 'This lamp will send its light for many miles out to sea. These prisms increase the strength of the light; it cost thousands of pounds to make this. Every day I have to clean these prisms and make sure the wick has enough oil because it needs to keep burning brightly. 'How does it move around Father?' George asked.

'All done by clockwork machinery, just like the clock in the living room moving the pointers. It flashes a light out to sea, every thirty seconds. Hopefully it will save lives, many lives. These rocks around here have cost many lives, do you know back in 1774, well a little over fifty years ago now, six ships crashed into these rocks in one day, costing over one hundred lives. They have fought for many years to get a light put here, well now they have one.' Father seemed happy. I looked out of the window, the sea was grey, the clouds were dark, it always worried me when the sky got dark, and I always worried about the sailors.

'Tonight will be the very first time the lamp is lit. It will be an historic occasion.' Father beamed.' We watched as he lit the the wick. The flame burned brightly, and the light hurt my eyes as it shone directly in my face. 'It's so powerful.' Brookes said, squinting. 'If you look outside you will see it casting its light across the sea, and it will even light up Brownsman Island.'

We all stepped outside onto the balcony, we waited for the light to turn, but after a few minutes we guessed something had gone wrong and went back inside. 'The wind blew out the flame.' Father said. 'Close the door behind you when you go out this time.' We carefully closed the door behind us and were rewarded with seeing the lamp flash its huge light out to sea. And just as he had said Brownsman Island was lit up for a few seconds, which delighted George and Brookes and they clapped their hands in glee. We must have stood outside for an hour watching the lamp revolving and flashing, lighting up the other Islands, it even lit up the castle at Bamburgh every 30 seconds. Father was so happy. 'Let us hope the ships heed the warning and it saves lives.' He said.

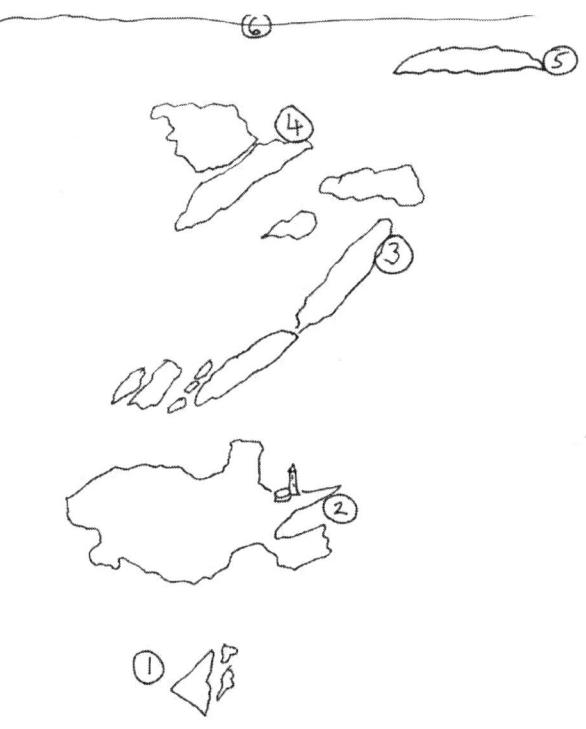

A map of the Farne islands.

1. Knavestone

2. Longstone Island

3. Big Harkers Rock

4. Brownsman Island

5. Inner Farne

6. The mainland

My drawing of our new home of Longstone Lighthouse and the barracks.

February 1st 1827

Almost a year has passed since we moved here, and things have changed a lot. Job, Thomasina and Mary have moved out. Job went to work as an apprentice Mason in Belford. Mary and Thomasin have gone to live with our Cousins in Bamburgh. Thomasin has set up her own dressmaking business and Mary is helping her. I miss them dearly. William came home with some wood and made a bed for Robert, so they now have a bed each. George has the top bunk, Brookes the bottom bunk and Robert has his own bed now. Betsy sleeps on the top bunk in our room, and I on the bottom. It is a lot quieter now they have left. Although George and Brookes help fill the house with laughter and cheer.

It's father's birthday tomorrow, I had ordered him a new snuff box and was expecting it on the goods delivery ship today, but the sea has been rough, and the ship wasn't able to come. Mother was unhappy too, because she had ordered some flour and sugar to make some cakes. I am worried because I have nothing to give him for his birthday. I have been outside looking for some bird's eggs, because I know he likes to collect them, but it's the wrong time of year, the breeding season hasn't started yet, and I couldn't find anything useful to give him. I am toying with the idea of making him a flute. I found a manual belonging to William, about making things with wood, and there are instructions in there to make a flute. You need a stick of bamboo, and a hot poker to burn a hole in the wood. Mother is always near the fire spinning or cooking, and I know if I asked to use the poker to burn holes in the wood she would say no. Little Brookes burned himself badly when he was little when he picked up the poker and imitated mother and stuck it in the hot coals, he grabbed the red glowing tip and burned his fingers so badly he still has scars on his finger tips. I shall have to wait until she leaves the room. I have already found some bamboo, it was used by Robert as a fishing rod, but it broke, and he said I could have it. I have very carefully followed the instructions of marking where the holes go. I need to make each hole an inch apart, and one hole an inch from the closed bottom end, a total of seven holes. I first need to use the poker to burn a hole through the fibrous wood inside the bamboo, and once that's done to make the holes. If mother doesn't leave the room for ten minutes, I am going to have to disappoint Father by not having anything to give him for his birthday.

I am writing this whilst mother is spinning her yarn. She is happy I am writing, and she respects my privacy and hasn't seen the contents of this book. Father has been teaching me to write. He has made the store room on the top floor into a school room. I love his lessons. Yesterday he taught me about St Cuthbert. St Cuthbert became a Bishop and used to be in charge of the monastery on Holy Island. He became famous for healing the sick, people came from all corners of the world to be healed by him, and receive his blessing. Even when St Cuthbert moved to live on Inner Farne Island, people flocked to the Island in their boats to see him. He lived just a few miles away from this Island, we can see Holy Island clearly from here and Inner Farne is south of Brownsman Island, and there is also a lighthouse on that Island too now, but not as bright as ours. St Cuthbert's life back then in the 7th century would have been very similar to our lives here today. He lived on an Island home, suffered the same types of weather, and stormy seas, and I bet his Island was flooded too on occasions. He grew wheat and barley, as my father does on Brownsman Island. He loved the animals, seals, and a wide variety of birds made their home there. There are stories of how the seals dried his feet with their warm breath. And he loved Eider ducks too so much that he helped to make laws to protect them. He would have loved my Cussy. It was though very sad to hear how he died, the weather had been bad, and the monks used to row out to take him his food and water, but because of the weather no-one was able to get to him for five days. They found him very ill in bed having only onions to eat. He died soon after. They moved his body to Chester Le Street, but it now rests in Durham Cathedral. It does worry me sometimes living on an Island, what if we have bad weather for days and can't get food, what will happen to us? We also rely on people bringing us water; they bring it in barrels from the mainland. We have enough water to last us a week, so I hope this storm doesn't last more than a week. Father says he will row us to the mainland if he had to, so not to worry, but I can't help worrying about it, and now hearing that story about St Cuthbert has made me worry a bit too much I fear.

Father was also teaching me my times tables today. I know my 2s, 3s, 4s, 5s, 6s, 9s, 10s, and 11s, but I'm still struggling with learning my 7s, 8s, and 12 times tables. We chanted them for an hour this morning, but my mind was on the storm. I could see the black clouds building and could see the surf hitting the rocks. The waves were getting higher. This Island isn't as high as Brownsman Island. It is only a metre above sea level, and Brownsman was three metres above sea level, so it is likely to be flooded like we were that time, and the waves have covered most of the Island more than once this year, I fear tonight could be another such occurrence. I fear I shall not sleep tonight, but at least I am on the third floor, much higher than when I was on Brownsman, and I am sure the waves will not reach this height.

Mother has gone to check on the boys. I will try to make my flute now.

February 2nd 1827

I was holding the hot poker very carefully, I had a thick cloth to hold it with, and had managed to burn the hole inside the bamboo, and was about to burn the seven holes into the wood when my mother came in, saw me with the poker, and screamed so loud I dropped it. It landed on my foot and burnt my big toe on my right foot. It was very painful, I screamed. My mother quickly put my foot in a bucket of cold water, but even though the water was cold, it felt hot on my burn. My Father, brothers and sister all came running to see what had happened. When I heard them coming down the stairs, I hid my flute in my skirt. 'Don't tell Father, please mother.' I whispered. Mother gave me a firm look and said nothing. 'What's happened?' shouted Father. 'I dropped the poker on my foot,' I said. 'What were you doing with the poker, you know you haven't got to touch that?' said Father. He glared at my mother thinking she had neglected her duties and allowed me to be feckless with dangerous items. 'I was upstairs seeing to the boys,' she said. Mother put small white linen dressing on, and I gave her a big hug for not telling father. She even helped me make the holes in the flute after Father had gone back to the lantern, and the others had gone back to bed. We had to go outside in the dark to hunt for a rough stone to smooth the rough edges and scrap away the charcoaled bit made by the hot poker. It was very windy, and part of the Island was flooded, so mother wouldn't let me go more than a few feet away from the tower, she said I could very easily get swept away out to sea if a wave suddenly washed over us. I did manage to find a perfect rough stone that was thin on one end. Mother helped me sand down the flute with the stone I couldn't test it out though because Father would have heard it, and then it would have spoiled the surprise.

I hardly slept a wink last night, as my toe was painful, and the noise of the wind and the surf kept me awake. I could feel my bed vibrate every time the waves lashed at the rocks, and the wind was howling outside, the rain pelted against my window. I worried in case there were ships out to sea, and worried in case they couldn't see the light for the spray. I got up and tried to look out of the window but Betsy told me to get back to bed as it was the middle of the night.

So this morning I woke up really tired. I was though so excited for Father to open my present and play his new flute.

I ran downstairs to the living room, Betsy followed me, but mother came out of the room and stopped us going downstairs. 'It's flooded.' She said in a quiet hushed voice. 'The whole of the living room is flooded. We are waiting for the tide to drop and then we will all have to help clear the living room of the water. Your father is sleeping at the moment; he has been tending to the light all night. So go back to your room and I'll come for you in an hour or so.' I could see the water lapping the bottom stairs. I was so glad our room was higher up. 'Are the boys okay?' I asked. 'Yes your father has been keeping a check on them all night. Luckily the water only entered the living room.'

I went back upstairs feeling like my heart was so heavy it would just burst. I was so looking forward to wishing Father a Happy Birthday, and then we didn't even have a living room we could enter. What an awful day for him to be having his birthday, a flooded home, no cakes, and even William, Job, Mary and Thomasin cannot visit him because of the weather. Betsy climbed back into her bed, and I climbed back into mine. I soon fell fast asleep and was woken with Father's cheery voice singing. Betsy heard it too, and we ran downstairs to their room to find the boys already there. 'Happy Birthday Father!' Betsy and I said in unison. We all gave him our presents. When he got to mine he played with it for a bit, he was really puzzled by the shape. 'Is it a cigar?' he asked. I shook my head laughing. Then when he opened it he gasped in surprise. 'A flute, I have always wanted a flute, where did you buy it?' He asked.

'Oh that's a secret,' I said. I looked at Mother and she smiled at me. He picked the flute up and put it to his lips and was about to blow, when Brookes asked him how old he was. 'I am forty one year's young, ' he laughed.

I waited as he put the flute to his lips again. 'How old are you Mother?' Brookes asked. 'Oh you are not supposed to ask a lady her age Brookes you should know that,' said Father. 'Please mother, how old are you now?'

'Fifty two dear.'

'So that means you are older than Father,' he said. 'Yes, but...'

'Your mother looks younger than I, don't you think? And more beautiful. Age is just a number really, I married your mother for her sweet nature, and delightful sense of humour, and I would marry her all over again given the chance.' He put the flute to his mouth and blew. A beautiful tune then resonated around the room. He stopped playing and smiled a big wide smile. 'What a beautiful gift. Thank you so much Grace,' He hugged me and kissed me on the head, then began playing again. The music filled everyone's hearts with the melody, and soon we were all dancing around the room to the music. Forgetting our home was flooded for a moment. Music is a blessing; it fills our hearts with joy, thank God for music.

We spent the rest of the morning chatting with Father before he had to go and row to Brownsman Island to check on the animals. Robert went with him, whilst the rest of us all helped to sweep the water from the living room and clean the whole room. It took almost all day, then we sat down to dinner, and father played his flute some more and we danced and sang.

My drawing of the flute.

December 24th 1830

It is Christmas Eve. I have been so busy there has been very little time to write in my diary. I am fifteen years old now and we have lived here now for nearly five years. I help my father and my mother now with their tasks. I sometimes look after the lantern, and allow father some much needed sleep, as Robert is now boarding at the castle at the school there.

This Christmas will be melancholy. We had been so excited for this Christmas. We were all going to be together as a family again. William was coming home, and Job was returning, Robert was coming home, and Mary and Thomasin were coming to stay over Christmas. Father had even fixed the roof on the barracks and put in some mattresses for William and Job. And I had helped mother make it look homely. We made some beautiful curtains for the window, and some lovely quilts for their beds. Then we got the telegram. Job had taken ill and would not be coming home. He was so poorly he had to be taken to the Infirmary in Newcastle. Mother and Father went to visit him there and when they came home I knew something terrible had happened. Mother's eyes were swollen with crying, and her expression was one of sorrow. Father too had been crying and he had his arm around mother as they came up the path. She was dabbing her face with her handkerchief. 'What's happened?' I asked, partly knowing what they were going to say. They didn't answer at first. Father took mother to their room then came downstairs and told us to sit down. George, Brookes and I sat waiting for the terrible news to spill forth from his lips. Tears were already pricking my eyes as I feared the worst.

'Job was very poorly, he had an illness that they did not know how to treat, he got a fever, the Infirmary tried their best to save him, but they could not. Job is dead; he is with Jesus in heaven.' Father started crying as he said those words, and so did we all. Mother was also crying. I could hear her howls from her room. Father hugged us all to comfort us, but hugging did not bring relief to the sorrow in my heart. Job was dead, my brother, my dear brother, who was so looking forward to coming home for Christmas, and spending his twentieth birthday here, was now dead, and with the Lord in heaven. I would never see him again. I thought back to how he saved my life when we had the flood on Brownsman, he was a good boy, he was sensible, and he was doing well working as a Mason, his boss had been full of praise for him, he was only nineteen years old. It was such terrible news; the house has not been the same since. Father has not picked up any instrument; there is no singing in the house. We still cry every day when we think about him. Christmas Day tomorrow is not going to be joyful at all. I asked Father if he would cancel Christmas this year, but he would not entertain the Idea. 'It's not what Job would have wanted, he would have wanted us to celebrate his life, and that is what we are going to do tomorrow. We will give thanks to God for allowing us to have the years we had with Job.'

Father always said the right thing; he always tried to make the positive out of the negative. Tomorrow we will go to Bamburgh; William is taking us on a big boat he borrowed from his client. We will celebrate the birthday of Jesus and the time we shared with Job. It will be a special day. We will give praise to Jesus in St Aidan's church in Bamburgh, then visit Job's grave, before returning to the

Island for Christmas lunch. It will be a sorrowful day without him.

June 5th 1832

It has been an exciting day today. Firstly we were all given the very good news that Mary Ann was to be married, to George Dixon Carr, we knew it was coming, but the news just sent waves of joy over me. I am so happy for them, it's put everyone in good spirits, we have been talking nonstop about the wedding ever since. Then this afternoon, my father took me to Brownsman Island for the sheep shearing. Mac was in charge of the shearing, and he asked me if I wanted to have a go. Of course I said yes. But he is being very trusting of a sixteen year old girl. I watched Mac shear a sheep first and he talked me through it.

'Just keep their feet off the floor and they won't struggle,' Mac said. 'Pull their head between your legs and hold him with your knees, then taking the shears snip as closely to the skin as you can. When you come up the belly, hold his nose while you snip under his chin.'

I watched as the skilful sheep shearer presented his newly shorn sheep. The fleece was heavy and in one piece and he lifted it up with pride. 'Come on now girl, it's your turn.'

Mac brought out a sheep and he looked at me with his cute scared eyes. 'Now grab his fur and pull him backwards towards you.' Mac said. Father smiled as if he knew I couldn't do it. I grabbed his fur and pulled him backwards, but the sheep got away and started running towards Mac. Father stopped it and brought it towards me. Mac took hold of it and pulled it backwards till it lay on its back like a beetle kicking its legs. Then he pulled it up towards my skirt and I grabbed hold of its fur. Its fur was very thick. Mac passed me the shears. And I carefully tried to snip away the fur from the side of its neck. The sheep struggled, so I stopped snipping. I was scared in case I cut his skin which was now visible from the area I'd snipped. 'Hold him closer to you, nip your legs on his body,' he said. I did as I was told and the sheep stopped struggling. I began snipping carefully down the side of its neck then along its front. The fur began peeling back to reveal a pinkish whitish skin. I continued snipping down his back until I couldn't reach any further. I was unsure of how to cut the fur under his back. I looked up to ask Mac what to do. He was gone, he and father were chasing after a sheep that was getting too close to the edge of the rocks. I looked down at the sheep again, he looked up at me as if to say, are you finished yet? I tried to change my position so I could snip down the other side of his neck, and as I was moving the sheep struggled violently, I grabbed him and tried to pull him back, but he moved again. Fortunately, he moved so I could cut down his other side. I began snipping down the other side of his neck, then without warning he jumped up. The shears nicked his skin and blood started oozing from a cut on his neck staining his fur red. I jumped back in horror and the sheep darted off towards Mac dragging his fleece behind him. Mac caught him and brought him back to me. 'You are doing grand job lass, look you have gave him a little nick, don't worry about that, it's just a pin prick, you are almost half way there.' Mac held the sheep for me and I continued shearing until the full fleece fell away from him. Mac picked up the fleece and gave it a shake. Dust filled the air, and it made me cough. 'Look, what a marvellous job, you can come and work for me anytime.' He handed me the fleece. It still felt warm. The sheep galloped off looking happy he didn't have to wear that fur coat in the blazing sunshine.

We rowed back to Longstone with the fleeces, mother was surprised to be given so many fleeces, she loves spinning and she told me that would keep her busy for weeks. I will spin my fleece, then I will dye the wool, and I'll use it to knit father a new jumper.

My head is still full of the memories from today. I now need to help mother in making preparations for Mary Ann's wedding. Mary said she would like us to make her wedding gown. I am so excited, I have started making designs.

Mary said she wanted a big flowing skirt, and would wear hoops underneath, and a bodice tight at the waist. She wanted it made in white silk, with pearls and lace. In my first design I have made it with ruffled lace around the neckline, there will be beads around the the v in the dropped waist, and beads in the neckline. The skirt will be full and flowing, and the veil will be of delicate lace.

Design 1.

Design 2

The second design would have a full skirt, with lace overlay, ruffled and in layers. A beaded waist and no sleeves. I will carry on designing; mother and I will show her our designs next week and see what she says. They are to be married in November at St Aidan's Church. She wants Thomasin, Betsy and I to wear pink, but I haven't even thought of those designs yet, we are going to be so busy over the coming months. I also help Father with his lantern duties, and I now row to Brownsman to attend to the animals and crops to help father. The family will be here together again. Except Job, but I hope he will be watching from heaven.

Mary said she will be married on 18th November. The saying goes,

> *Marry on Monday for health,*
> *Tuesday for wealth,*
> *Wednesday the best day of all,*
> *Thursday for crosses,*
> *Friday for losses, and*
> *Saturday for no luck at all.*

The 18th of November is a Sunday, yet there is no rhyme for the Sunday, I am worrying about that, mother says I worry too much, and she knows of lots of people who have married on a Sunday. She says it is the only day when we can all be together as William and Robert are both working throughout the whole week and cannot get time off. I worry in case it brings them bad luck. But I cannot have time for worrying, I need to sleep now, I am exhausted it has been such a busy day.

25th December 1832

What an exciting day it has been today. Christmas Days are normally exciting but today has been ultra exciting.

We were just getting over the excitement of Mary Ann's wedding, it was a wonderful wedding, Mary looked just beautiful in her wedding dress. We ended up with twenty designs, and she chose this one.

Design 17

She looked like a princess. It was made from white satin, and it had very pale pink flowers sewn into the frill on the skirt. Her corset was pulled tight at the back so she could hardly breathe; the frilly lace bodice was so pretty. Her hair was all ringlets, mother had spent the evening before the wedding wrapping her hair around the braid to make the ringlets and they turned out beautifully. George wore a divine black suit with waistcoat, and top hat, he looked so handsome.

My mother said it was tradition to wear something old, something new, something borrowed, something blue, and have a silver sixpence in her shoe.

I put the silver sixpence in her shoe, and she borrowed a pearl necklace from mother, the dress was new, and she was given a blue garter to wear under her dress. Mother's necklace was old so she said it counted for both old and borrowed.

It took a while for Mary to decide what our bridesmaid dresses should be, here is the design she chose.

Our dresses were made from pink satin, and we also had the pink flowers sewn into the skirt. It was such a beautiful ceremony. Mother was crying, and so was I. It was good to have all the family round us once again; it gets so lonely sometimes on the Island.

So today was extra special because we had one more to cook for, and George is so funny, he fits in so well with the rest of the family, he kept us all entertained he did. But they have also given us some extra exciting news, Mary

Ann is now pregnant, that means I am going to be an aunt. It will be strange having a young child call me Aunt Grace, but it will be very special. I am going to start knitting baby clothes; I can't wait for the baby to arrive.

28th December 1834

Last night my father and my brothers almost lost their lives. I spotted a sloop against Knavestone rock, and could just make out the figure of a man standing. I was watching the lantern as Father had gone to rest; I had to wake him urgently. He jumped up and taking William, Robert and George went to their rescue. I was getting worried when they didn't return. They had been gone for hours. It was hard to see. I had watched them row to the rock in the cobble, but they seemed to be spending a long time near the rock. I worried in case they were stuck. Mother was sleeping and I didn't want to wake her, because I know how much it affects her, she would be past herself.

Then I caught sight of the sail. I was puzzled why they were using the sail; they could have rowed back, so I knew something must have happened with the oars.

I was waiting for them when they docked. They had a young man with them, James Logan. He had been delivering coal from Sunderland in a sloop. He was almost unconscious when he arrived, Father said he had leaped from the rock which was partly covered with the tide, into the boat, and had slept all the way back. He was icy cold and shivering, his teeth were chattering when we carried him inside. We lay him near the fire to help warm him up, stripped him of his wet clothes, and put him to bed and covered him well with warm blankets. He woke up eight hours later to tell us the tale of what happened. He said they hit the rock, which was invisible as the water was covering it; the ship began listing on its side, so James and his friend climbed up the mast. When the tide went out, they were able to jump onto the rock, but sadly their master had died. He said his boots had filled with water and he couldn't climb the mast, he went down with the ship under the water. His friend fell asleep on the rock, and they stayed there for hours, then the tide started coming back in again, and the water swept him off the rock into the sea.

George said it was a dangerous mission. The danger of it was the boat they were in was getting dangerously near to the rock, and if it had struck the rock they would have all surely perished. So they had to row backwards away from the rock when the waves were pushing them towards it, and row forwards when the waves were pushing them away from it. It was hard work just keeping the boat near the rock without hitting it. James was waist high in water, as the tide was covering the rock again. When he saw the boat couldn't get close enough for him to climb in, he leaped with all his might, and landed in the boat flat on his face. But even after he was in the boat, the danger wasn't over, they were jammed close near to the rocks and they couldn't get away from them. So they used the oars to try and push the boat away from the rocks, but going against the waves pushing them at the same time. Their oars snapped. They were stuck against the rock without oars to row, and the waves were pushing them harder against the rocks. Robert said he feared for all their lives. He and George then jumped into the icy cold waters to try and free the boat. They put their own lives in danger, as the current was very strong, and the sea in December was freezing. They managed to free the boat from the rocks, and father and William helped them back into the boat. The only thing they could do then was to hoist the sail, and pray the wind would carry them home. But the wind was going in the wrong direction. They prayed to God, and by a miracle the wind changed and it carried them back to Longstone. It was a sheer miracle they returned. We gave praise to God.

We had some more good news today. Mary is pregnant again. We were so sad when she lost her baby last year, but now we are delighted for her again.

1st January 1838

New Years Day. We had a lovely time last night. The whole family was here for the celebrations. The family is getting bigger now that Mary Ann, Betsy, and William have all been married. It's getting harder to squeeze everyone in the living room at once, so last night we went to The Victoria Hotel in Bamburgh to celebrate, and we stayed the night at Thomasin's. George offered to watch the lantern. We partied till 2am and then slept till ten.

Mary Ann is happy to be pregnant again, but worried at the same time. She is beginning to think she is cursed after she lost her second baby. But we have all been telling her, 'Third time lucky.' Betsy has a little boy now called James; he is eight months old, and so sweet. He is very inquisitive, and has begun crawling around. We have to be very careful what we put on the floor. He found Father's flute yesterday, and delighted in hearing it make a noise when he blew into it, so he kept playing the flute like a whistle. Father says he may grow up to be musical; we will have to wait and see.

It was wonderful having all of the family together again. It gets lonely sometimes here at Longstone. There is just Father, Mother and I left living here now. We do get visitors sometimes. Birdwatchers come to watch the birds, artists come to paint, and we do let them stay here sometimes in the boy's room. I enjoy having guests, but Father seems to enjoy the company even more. He enjoys telling his favourite ghost stories, or reading 'The Ancient Mariner' to them. He swears he has seen a ghost ship on the ocean, but I fear it may have been at a time he had been drinking too much ale. He said the ship floated above the rocks, it was white and transparent, then disappeared. The visitors appear to believe every word, and we find them looking out of the window for ghost ships. They do get scared, because the last visitor we had, I went to give him a cup of tea, he was staring out to the ocean, and when I tapped him on the shoulder he nearly jumped out of his skin. It was so funny I nearly dropped the cups laughing.

    Mother is getting old now, she is sixty three, and can't help as much as she used to with the housework, so I have to do it all myself. She still does her spinning and needlework though, which she enjoys, and she still enjoys cooking. But I find I am now having less free time to read, or relax. Its hard work here without the boys. When the boys were here they did some of the chores in the house, and they helped with looking after the animals at Brownsman, and looking after the crops. But now I find I am working all day. Father watches the lantern for half of the day or night, and I watch it for the other half. We have to clean the prisms and the lantern windows daily, and inspect for damage. Sometimes a duck or bird flies into the window. Once the lantern was broken when a duck flew in, we had to quickly order replacements. We did though have the duck for dinner that night. The wick needs attention, and we have to make sure there is enough oil.

    We also watch out for passing ships that could get stuck on the rocks. Even though the lantern is bright and shines for miles out to sea, sometimes accidents still happen, like at Knavestone rock. We have a telescope that was given to us by Trinity and we need to keep a close watch just in case there have been any wrecks. The Castle too keeps watch, and if they spot a wreck they fire their guns, to give a signal to any passing ships or to fishermen, that there are lives in danger. We haven't heard their guns for a long time now, so the light must be doing its job. It's hard at night to see in the dark, if the moon is full and there are no clouds in the sky we can see better, otherwise we rely on the light lighting up the rocks for a split second every thirty seconds.

Every day the animals need attending to on Brownsman Island. We have built shelters for them for the winter. Even the ducks have their own shelter. We had to build them new ones after the last storm because they were damaged. I need to milk the goats, and collect the eggs. It's good we do keep crops and animals there because often the goods ship doesn't arrive because of the weather, and if it wasn't for the milk and the eggs, our own crop of potatoes, carrots and barley, we may starve. But it does take up much of the day rowing out there and back again, I usually begin the housework after I have been to tend to the animals. Sometimes Mother looks after the lantern for a while, but her knees ache, and there are around a hundred steps to the top of the lighthouse, so we only ask her to do this if it is really necessary. Father sleeps for less than four hours sometimes, so he can take over from me, so I can attend to the animals. But he also rows to Brownsman, we take it in turns. If the weather is bad though we just go there when the storm has passed, I hate going after a storm because once I found all of the crops completely ruined as the sea had covered the Island, and washed the crops away, and some of the animals had been washed out to sea too, so it worried me going there after a storm; Father volunteers to do that for me usually. Our old house is just a ruin now. Part of the house has collapsed. The sea can be so strong and powerful, it can just flatten stones walls as if they were sticks. It's lucky we are not living there still; I watched the waves crashing over the top of the house last October though the telescope. It would have been very dangerous if we were all still living there. Our home here has been flooded a few times, and we have seen the waves reach as high as the boys room, but thankfully the lighthouse is a sturdy building, the walls are very thick, so far, touch wood, we have all been safe.

Time to row to Brownsman. Thankfully it is a beautiful sunny day, although very cold. I shall make sure to give the hens and ducks double corn to help keep them warm.

30th June 1838

It was Queen Victoria coronation on 28th June. We had a trip to Bamburgh to celebrate. Everyone was waving flags.

I saved a clipping from the newspaper.

THE CORONATION OF HER MAJESTY QUEEN VICTORIA.

BUCKINGHAM PALACE.

Yesterday, the day fixed upon for the coronation of her most gracious Majesty Queen Victoria the First, must be one for ever memorable to those who had the happiness of joining in its celebration, and of demonstrating the affection entertained by them for their Sovereign. It was a day of unmingled delight—a festival in which the finest tastes and the finest feelings were fully gratified. It was not a mere holiday which the humbler classes could hail as a "day of rest" from labour; nor even one in which they might indulge in innocent amusements; nor please the eye by gazing upon a mere gorgeous spectacle; but it was a national ovation, in which they were actors as well as the Sovereign: for while they hailed her as their Queen, they expressed at the same time the delight with which they looked upon her; and her Majesty expressed, not merely by action but by words, the love, the care, and the regard that she has for her people. We cannot give a stronger proof of this than an anecdote we heard related of her Majesty in the course of the day. A short time before her Majesty proceeded to her carriage, it has been stated, that upon its being observed that her Majesty must undergo a great deal of fatigue before the proceedings of the day were terminated, she said to one of her attendants, that "the greatest anxiety experienced by her was, that in the course of the day no accident might occur to any of her faithful subjects, whose loyalty to the throne and affection for their Sovereign might induce them to attend for the purpose of evincing their regard for her." Such a sentiment is quite in accordance with the demeanour and bearing of her Majesty. In both there is that joyousness and tenderness which youth alone can command, and a female only can give expression to.

This regiment is commanded by Colonel Thomas, M P. for Kinsale; but he was not with the regiment, or, if in the Park at all, he must have been in coloured clothes. The regiment was for the day under the command of Majors Hutchinson and Smart. A few minutes after seven o'clock a detachment of the 5th Dragoon Guards was placed at the Palace-gates, but in a short time afterwards removed, and their place supplied by the 2d Life Guards. Thus, when the procession set out, three lines were formed, the innermost line composed of the 30th regiment, the second line of the Life Guards, and the outermost line of the police, the E division forming that nearest to the palace. Even before the procession commenced the aspect of the various lines thus formed was exceedingly beautiful. Before the spectator was the palace thus invested with the troops and the people. There was the eagerness of the crowd on one side to obtain what they considered a good situation—the constant shifting of the vast multitude around the outermost rim of the circle—and the incessant moving of troops within it; while ever and anon a gorgeously dressed hussar, or a silver-cuirassed officer, seen darting within the lines, gave to the entire picture all the beauty and effect of a living panorama, in which there was nothing to be seen but what was pleasing, and nothing to be observed but that which was worthy of admiration. This was the spectacle at the palace; while, nearly upon a line with it, although concealed from its view by the shrubberies in the Park, was to be found an encampment half-way between the Horse-guards and the palace, and nearly opposite St. James's. The small encampment belonged to the Royal Artillery, who had nineteen tents erected, in front of which were drawn up twelve nine-pound pieces. Their duty was to fire a salute in honour of the occurrence of each successive event of importance during the day. During the morning we noticed, passing from one point to another in the Park, Major-General Sir Charles Dalbiac, who had the command of all the troops; the Master-General of the Ordnance, Sir Hussey Vivian; Sir George Quentin, who wore

Queen Victoria is the niece of King Edward 1V who died sadly last year. Our new Queen is younger than me. I pray she has God's blessing to rule our country.

6th September 1838

    A very strong gale is blowing. I can see the waves are higher than usual and are pounding against the rocks. Father and I have been out to tie up the cobble boat, and fasten the oars; we have boarded up the downstairs windows, and placed sandbags along the bottom of the doorway. Father said the gale is the strongest he has seen for a while, and said the tide is higher than usual. He worries in case there is going to be a tidal surge. He noticed the wind beginning to blow when he was at Brownsman, and secured the the animals taking them to the ruined house and putting them upstairs. He says it will be safer for them, and he has also given them extra corn and fresh water in case he is unable to get to them tomorrow. The storm looks like it is getting worse. When we were out the wind was so strong it knocked me backwards, and took my breath away. I had to turn so my back was against the wind, my skirt billowed out in front of me, I thought I was going to take flight at one stage. The wooden chair that was outside that my father had stood on to board the windows was picked up by the wind and threw against the rocks breaking it in two. Even inside we can hear the howling wind, and the windows are rattling. The rain has started now and the wind is blowing it horizontally. When I went out to check on the cobble, I felt the rain hitting my back so hard it felt like needles. I am wet through now and exhausted. Father has asked me to take over from him at 4am, so I need to get to bed early tonight, but it is now midnight, and I shall be lucky to have four hours sleep. The noise of the wind and rain is also preventing me from relaxing enough to fall asleep. I do hope there are no ships out there tonight in this.

7th September 1838

    I took over from father this Wednesday at 4am. The storm had worsened. I checked the rocks with the telescope as soon as I had attended to the light. I waited for the light to light up Brownsman Island, I was anxious to find out if the sea had covered it. I couldn't believe what I saw in the second the Island was lit. A large ship was against the rocks and was listing. My heart beat faster as I waited for the light to shine there again, I fear I may have been seeing things, but it soon became clear that there was a ship against the rocks. I quickly ran down to wake father, he had only been in bed forty five minutes. Father jumped up and went to look through the telescope.

    'It is too dark, I cannot see if there are people on the rock. It looks like the ship is cut in two and one half must have sunk, the other half is against the rocks. It is too dark know, we may have to wait for dawn to break before we can know any better.'

    'We must go to them Father, before it is too late, there may be people alive.'

    'We do not know yet whether there are any survivors. But the sea is far too rough, the waves are too high, and the wind is too mighty, if it can split apart a big ship like that, what could it do to a small rowing boat lass.'

    'But Father, we may be too late, what if we get there too late, lives could be lost.'

    'Our lives could be lost. It is far too dangerous to go out in that weather, and just the two of us. It took four of us to row out to knavestone for that wreck, there is only you and I, and you have never rowed in such seas, it takes a lot of strength to pull on those oars against the current, our oars were snapped like twigs the last time, it could happen again, and if it wasn't for the boys our lives could have been lost. Anyway it is far too dark, we need to be able to see to navigate around those hazardous rocks, and we have no moon light because of the thick black clouds, even if the wind and rain ceased, we cannot put out in a boat in such darkness, those rocks out there are a danger to us too, those waves could pick us up and dash us against the rocks, it is too risky. Now go and make us a hot cup of tea, and I will keep watch for a while.'

Father and I waited for the dawn to break. Checking continuously the wreck through the telescope. Then before seven I spotted some figures on the rock, there looked to be around four people. 'Father there are some survivors on the rock look!' I yelled. Father looked through the telescope. 'Indeed there are, but the storm hasn't abated and the waves are enormous, the wind is worse now than it was before. That ship looks like is has split in two.'

'But Father, we can see our way to navigate round the rocks now, the people are desperate, they could be swept to their deaths any moment, we have to go and save them Father, they are reliant on us, we need to go now Father before it is too late.'

Father looked me up and down as if doubting I had the strength to help him.

'Grace, you know this is a dangerous mission, we may not get back alive, the sea is too mighty even for experienced sailors and boatman at times, if you come with me, you need to do everything I say, pull the oar when I say, and when we get to the rock, I will have to leave you in the boat alone for a while, you will then have to prevent the boat from hitting the rock, if a wave pushes you towards the rock you will need to row backwards with all your might, and if you are pushed away front he rock you will need to bring the boat forward. It is a long way to Harkers Rock, we need to go round the long way to avoid the risk of the waves dashing us against the rocks in between here and Harkers, it will take us at least half an hour to row there, and in these stormy seas it takes a lot of strength and energy. Are you willing to take that risk?'

'No!' Mother interrupted. 'It's far too dangerous, are you mad? I fear I will lose a husband and a daughter, No let someone else rescue them.'

'The weather is too bad for even those in North Sunderland to try and help, if those lives are to be saved or lost, it is down to us Mother, we need to put our trust in God, he will help us with this mighty task Father.' I pleaded. I could not stand by and watch people die, God had instilled the need to rescue them, he was putting the responsibility of their lives on us. They must have prayed to God to ask for his help and he wanted to send us. I knew it was our duty to save them.

'Okay girl, put on some warm clothes, and a hat.' I hugged Father, and I hugged Mother. She was shaking her head, tears were in her eyes.

We went outside into the howling wind and lashing rain. The sky was black with clouds.

We untied the cobble, and with Mother's help we pushed the boat into the water. Father held it as I climbed aboard which wasn't easy because the boat was being bashed about by the waves, then father pushed it a bit further out and jumped inside. We each took an oar and rowed away from Longstone and out into the wild angry sea.

Mother went back inside, and I could see her tiny face looking out from my bedroom window as we rowed hard against the mighty waves.

I looked across to the rock where the wreck was, but the wind was lashing the rain against me, and the waves were too high for me to see over them. A gigantic wave swiftly moved towards us and we could do nothing in our power to avoid it. It was a high as a mountain, and as black as the clouds above. It lifted us high into the sky, I was fearful what the wave would do with us, and I gripped the oar with all my might in case I was flung from the boat. I felt my stomach flip as we were catapulted with great speed down the back of the wave, I felt as if I wanted to vomit. As we reached the valley between the waves, water poured over us, and I felt my shoes fill with water. There was water now inside the boat.

'Father! The boat is filling with water.' I yelled, but the sound of the wind and the roar of the sea was too great, my voice was unable to rise above it. The waves tossed us with great forth backwards and sideways, having no mercy. And again we were carried high into the sky with a wave as big, if not bigger than the last one. From my vantage point I could see the wreck. Half of the ship was wedged against the rock; the other half must have sunk. The wreck was still very far away. I looked to see if I could make out how many people there were, but found we were again hurtling down the wave with great speed.

Father looked back, and I managed to get his attention and pointed to the water at my feet.

'Don't worry; it will take more water than that to sink her. Just keep rowing.'

I pulled on the oar with both hands, but the water felt like it wanted to rip it away from me. My skin was wet and cold, and every piece of clothing was soaked through. A wave broke near the boat, and the spray burst upon me, soaking me again and taking my breath away. Father too was soaked, water dripped from his coat, but he never stopped rowing and urged me to do the same. I worried in case I didn't have enough strength, and would cause him suffering having to row harder to compensate for my weakness. I pulled on the oar in rhythm to Father's pull, and tried to pull as hard. I prayed to God as I rowed that the people would be saved and our lives to be spared. We were at God's mercy in a small boat in the fury of the wild ocean and mighty wind. I worried in case we were too late and find only the bodies of those poor souls if they had not been swept out to sea.

We we rewarded with the sound of cries for help, as we neared Harkers Rock, my heart leaped with delight knowing there were still some people alive. It gave me energy and we found the strength to row faster towards them. As we neared the wreck I could see the horror before me. Several bodies were floating in the sea around us. The look on their faces were looks I shall never forget. Some people were still clinging to the wreck, some were on the rocks, there were nine people that I could see. As we got closer the people started gathering on the edge of the rock. Some were laughing and singing praises to God, some were crying, a woman was howling. They looked like they were all going to leap into the boat at once. I worried because this would surely capsize the boat and all our lives would be lost. Father turned to me.

'Grace remember what I said, keep the boat near but not too close in case a wave pushes you against the rocks.' I nodded and he leapt onto the rocks above.

A wave caught the boat and pushed me towards the rock, I quickly started rowing backwards as Father had said, and watched as the waves crashed against the rocks, sending spray high into the air. Then I felt I was being swept away by the current and had to quickly row forwards before being pushed towards the rock again. I was constantly rowing backwards and forwards while Father tied a rope around a young woman. I helped get the boat as close as I could do so. I could see now that the ship had indeed been split in two, it was a large modern steamboat, the first of its kind, and the sea had ripped it in half. The bodies floating were great in number, and I could see several bodies inside a watery grave in the wreck, which was filled with water. The sight was disturbing but I tried to concentrate at the task in hand. I know it is a sight I will never forget. I then stood up in the boat to try to help the lady aboard which wasn't easy as the waves were rocking it severely from side to side. Father held tight onto the rope as she stepped from the rock onto the boat. She collapsed in a heap at my feet, sobbing and crying. 'My children, my children!' She yelled. I didn't know whether they had been swept out to sea, or whether they were alive on the rock. I trusted Father to rescue them if he was able. The next person passed down to me was a young man, he too looked distressed, and he too collapsed at my feet. He looked up to the sky and gave thanks to God. Then he hugged me and kissed me on the hand. He helped Father with three men into the boat. Then Father climbed in, leaving four people on the rock.

'We will take these five back to the Lighthouse, then return for the others. You look after Mrs Dawson Grace, her children were dead, we had to leave them on the rock. Now you men help me row this boat back to the lighthouse, the quicker we get back, the quicker we can save the others.'

The three men took the oars, to help Father. I comforted Mrs Dawson, she was too upset to speak, but I gave her my shoulder to rest on, and she cried into my shoulder as I hugged her. I was crying too, so many dead, some of them must have suffered great injuries when the ship hit the rock. One man's leg was deformed, and he had bleeding cuts. Mrs Dawson was in tremendous pain, she was badly injured, but all she could think of was her poor children.

When we arrived back at the lighthouse we found mother waiting for us. She hugged us both as we stepped from the boat, she said she had fainted when she saw a huge wave swallow us up, she thought we had been drowned, as she did not see us again after the wave went over us. She was so happy to see us she was crying with joy. She helped us help the others from the boat. Some of them were limping due to their injuries. We sat Mrs Dawson and the badly injured man near the warm fire, and mother served them warm bread and cocoa. Then Father went back to the rock taking two men with him to rescue the others.

Our living room became full. Mother and I were kept busy tending to their wounds as they told us the story.

Later Brookes arrived on a boat from North Sunderland with another six men. He said he had heard the cannons from the castle warning of the wreck but he had to travel five miles in the rough seas and gales, and did not get to the rock until 10am. He did not know we had rescued the survivors, and they went to the rock, and found the dead bodies of Mrs Dawson's two children, and found the body of a man. They moved the bodies higher up the rock to prevent them being thrown back into the sea, and then headed for the lighthouse for safety as the sea was too rough to make it back to North Sunderland. So now we have the nine survivors and Brookes, and six men from his boat. Mother is worried we shall not have enough food to feed them. There is a goods boat due today but it won't come in this weather, and there is no telling how long the next delivery will be, so she says we need to be careful with the food. She is going to make soup today, and she has enough flour to make some bread, that should last a day or two, so hopefully we may have enough for everyone.

      Father said the survivors will have to stay in the barracks. There are no beds in the Barracks now, so we have tried to make it comfortable putting down some hay for them to sleep on. But there is still a danger in case the Island gets flooded. The survivors are so grateful for a roof over their heads and to be safe from the tempestuous weather, that they don't mind where they sleep. Brookes will sleep in his room with some of the men from his boat, who have offered to sleep on the floor in his room. There is nowhere for Mrs Dawson to sleep, so I offered up my bed for her. When Mary Ann moved out she took the bunks and gave me a single bed in its place. The poor woman is distraught and in pain, with so many injuries. I think she will need to go to the infirmary at the castle tomorrow when the seas are calmer. Tonight I will sleep on the table in the living room. I am worried about sleeping on the floor in case we get flooded again.

8th September 1838

I cannot sleep. The memory of those faces in the water is haunting me. Every time I close my eyes I see their faces, the look of horror in their eyes still disturbs me. I am writing this by candle light. It is now 2am. Mrs Dawson must be asleep for all is quiet in the house. I could still hear her crying at 1am. The haunting sounds of her cries are so upsetting; I shall never forget the events of yesterday for as long as I live.

From the wreck I learned that at least forty three people lost their lives, and among our nine survivors four are named John. John Kidd a fireman, John McQueen a coal trimmer from Dundee, John Tulloch a carpenter from Dundee and John Nicolson a fireman from Dundee. The other survivors are Mrs Sarah Dawson a passenger, Daniel Donovan a fireman from Dundee, James Kelly a weaver, and Thomas Buchanan a baker from Dundee. Most of the passengers were too upset to talk to us about the event, but Daniel Donovan explained to us in detail what had happened. He said the ship was not sea worthy, and that they had leaky boilers. The ship was large a hundred and thirty two feet in length and twenty feet wide. It was a side paddle steam ship, and Daniel boasted it had the power of one hundred and ninety horses. Captain John Humble was in charge, and he had his wife with him for the journey from Hull to Dundee. Sadly he and his wife were drowned when the other half of the ship sank. The ship sailed every Wednesday from Hull to Dundee and it left Hull at 6:30pm on Wednesday 5th September. Daniel said the boilers began leaking during the night, and he told the captain he thought they should turn back, but he said the captain refused to turn back. Then the following night the boilers stopped working altogether, and they had no steam and no engine power. The fierce storm had begun, and the wind was gale force, yet the captain decided to hoist the sails. He had hoped to steer the ship along the fairway between Inner Farne and North Sunderland, but had mistaken our lighthouse on Longstone for the lighthouse on Inner Farne, it was a dangerous mistake to make, because the waters south of Longstone are full of hazardous rocks, a lot different from the waters south of Inner Farne.

     Daniel said the vessel struck the rock at around 4am. He said the sea then lifted the boat up into the air like a toy, then threw it against the rocks and smashed it in two. One half of the ship sunk immediately with the people inside. Some of the crew managed to launch a lifeboat and one of the passengers leaped into the boat. Daniel said he was on the wrong side of the wreck, to reach the boat, but he watched it row away with nine people on board. He said the other half of the wreck stuck fast against the rocks, but was filling with water. He helped get some of the people out and and in a safe place, but some clung to the wreck, and some climbed onto the rock. Mrs Dawson and her children were struck by a wooden beam, and he thinks this is what killed her children, and why she was so injured. He said her two children James aged seven and Matilda aged five died in her arms. But he said the cold wet weather didn't help either, and they may have died due to the cold. This made me feel really guilty, if Father and I had rowed out to the wreck in the night at 5am we may have saved them poor children, it worried me to think their lives were lost and had they may have been saved. It breaks my heart. I keep crying when I think of it.

     Daniel and some of the others found the reverend John Robb, in the engine room, but he too was dead, they carried him onto the rock to save his body from being swallowed by the sea. Whilst they were on the rock, they were being continually covered by the waves lashing over the rocks, and sometimes they were pushed off the rocks by the water and had to swim frantically to get back onto them. Some of their clothes had been torn from them.

10th September 1838

The weather had not abated for three days, so we needed to tend to our guests for three days before Mr Smeddle, the governor from Bamburgh Castle was able to organise transport to take the survivors to the Infirmary in the Castle. Mrs Dawson's condition deteriorated whilst she was here, she developed a fever so I am glad she is now in the Infirmary where they can give her better care.

The goods ship arrived with delight this morning. Mother had to ration the food, and the guests were more needy than we, so we ate less than normal. My dress feels a little loose today; I think I have lost some weight. Mother is going to make my favourite apple tart tonight.

It has been so busy these last few days; I have hardly had time to think. I have had so many different jobs to do. I have helped mother with the cooking, we were used to having a large family before my brothers and sisters left home, but we had to cook for eighteen people, we just didn't have pots big enough, so we had to make two batches of food, which meant we were over the stove all morning. Then there was extra washing to do, more plates to wash, and cutlery, cups, and we also had more clothes to wash. The house needed cleaning, and also the barracks and I have also been a nurse, tending to wounds and dressings. I think it is the busiest few days I have ever had in my life. The house is quiet again now, but we are expecting visitors later. Father said the house needs to be spotless, so it is going to be a busy day today.

Father managed to go to Brownsman, he said the animals are okay and have let them out onto the grass again. He says the house needs cleaning though.

11th September 1838

Mr Smeddle from Bamburgh Castle visited yesterday, with Mr Sinclair an agent from Berwick to assess the wreck, Mr Jordan Evans, a customs officer, and some men from the press. They were firing questions at father and I, they wanted to know about the exact rescue, the time we left in the cobble, the time we reached them, the people we rescued, the time we got back, how long they were here, the state of the weather. They wanted to know the route we took. I had to draw them a map.

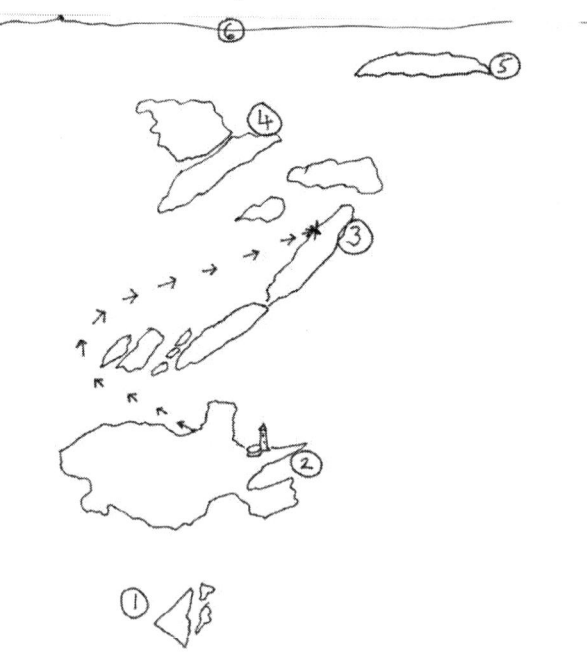

Father did most of the talking. He told them we had to stay south of the rocks to help get some shelter from the tides and the currents. The waves were enormous and staying south of the rocks meant we were put at less risk. It took longer to get there than a straight route though. They were also asking about the nine people who put out in the lifeboat. They had been rescued and taken to Tynemouth but we didn't know anything about that. Mr Smeddle praised me saying he was very pleased I had shown such extreme bravery. I found myself blushing, I hope he didn't notice. I was not used to the attention, so many men wanting to know about me. Mr Smeddle joked that there would be a silk gown for me for my bravery. I don't want a reward for helping those people, neither does Father, we considered it our duty, and God's will to go to their rescue, but if God chooses to reward us somehow, then it shall be accepted, but to get a reward in such circumstances seems wrong to me, when so many died, we didn't save all of them.

Mr Smeddle said he had heard from Daniel Donavan that the Captain was at fault, and he seemed angry and said he would hold an inquest on Tuesday to get to the bottom of it. We do not need to go to the inquest, for which I am glad, he said the inquest would be about the ship and whether it was seaworthy and whether the Captain was negligent.

Time to go to Brownsman now to clean the house. I dread to think what condition it is in as the animals have been cooked up in there for four days.

30th September 1838

    This has been the worst month of my life. I never dreamed that helping someone could result in so much attention. I feel like I am being smothercated. Every day we have new visitors. Sometimes these visitors are members of the press, or government officials, or artists. So many people wanting to know about me. I have a sack full of letters asking me for locks of my hair. People are sending me gifts, sending me money, books, and other gifts. The newspapers have glorified the story, making me out to be a heroine. They have placed me firmly on a pedestal, and see me as some sort of idol. I am just an ordinary girl who helps Father look after the lighthouse. I helped row the boat to save some people, but anyone in my position would have done the same I am sure. I don't understand all of the attention. My time now is spent posing for artists. I think I have posed for at least ten different artists this week. They even impose on my father and my mother too. We need to pose in one position for ages, my body aches trying to hold the poses they want. My sisters have offered at times to pose in my place and we almost fooled one artist when Mary Ann pretended to be me. It was only after he started the drawing did he realise we had played a trick on him, if Mary Ann hadn't started laughing every time he called her Grace we may have fooled him completely. It was funny though; I pretended to be Mary Ann and stood watching him draw her. Father wasn't very happy when he found out, in fact he hit the roof, but hopefully he will understand now how much time it takes and how it takes me away from my work, and maybe he will turn them away in future.

We sometimes need to pose for family portraits such as this one.

What I hate the most is talking to the press. They all ask the same questions and it gets very tiresome repeating the whole story every ten minutes. Mary Ann defended me once and told them if they wanted the answers to the questions they only needed to read yesterday's newspaper. My life feels like it will never be the same again. I used to enjoy the peace and tranquillity of the islands, of course I got lonely at times, but for the most part was happy with living here, and happy with my work.

The press don't understand why I would want to live here. They try to make me feel abnormal for enjoying this tranquil lifestyle. But I have lived here since I was ten years old, I am now 22 years old, that's twelve years, and before that lived on Brownsman Island, so Island life is what I am used to, it's how I have grown up, yet the press seem to want to put the idea in my head that I should want to live a fast paced life on the mainland. I blame them for all of the visitors. If they had not glorified me so in the newspapers, people wouldn't be coming here to ask for locks of my hair, or want me to pose for paintings. They all seem to want to make money off me, like I am some kind of product. They have even started putting my picture on sweets and chocolate to try and sell their wares.

Father said it will pass when they find someone new to write about. I hope he is right.

Even the Duke of Northumberland requested we visit him in Alnwick Castle. He had received a letter from Mr Scafe, praising me, and the Duke wanted to meet us. He said we deserved recognition for our bravery, but although very kind, we do not want recognition, and prefer to carry on with our lives the way we used to. There aren't enough hours in the day to do my normal chores without having to stop for tourists, or artists, or the press. And as the letters flood in, it is taking me a long time to reply. The ink dries quickly on the paper and need to dip my quill before every word, it takes me a long time to write a letter, and I have hundreds to reply to. That day I also received a gift of £50 from Queen Victoria.

When we visited the Duke in Alnwick, there were so many people crowding round, in fact I would say thousands of people were there to take a look at me. They were grabbing at my clothes like they used to do to Jesus. They were calling my name, and asking me for locks of my hair. They began pushing and shoving as they jostled for better positions so they could see me pass by, but their pushing became too much, and it frightened me, I felt like we were going to be crushed. We were stuck in the crowd for what seemed like a lifetime before we were eventually rescued by the Duke's men and taken to Alnwick Castle. It must have been in the press, and as the artists had published their portraits of me, they knew who I was, and I couldn't escape them.

I have now so many thank you letters to write, and Mr Smeddle has given me lots of cards to sign, at least a hundred of them.

Father said he will help me when he can, but he too is so busy, and so is Mother.

I hope all of this attention dies down soon.

One of the prints of the portraits of me.

An artist painted this picture of my mother, father and I pushing the boat out to sea before the rescue. The artist was called James Wilson Carmichael, but Father called him John.

Here is a cutting from the Morning Chronicle of Friday 28th September 1838.

Seems my blushes didn't escape them.

Here is another column from the same paper.

> **GRACE DARLING.**
>
> The only impulse which could have actuated Grace Darling to the heroic conduct she displayed was that feeling of pity which is natural to a mind whose generosity and philanthropy are universal in their application, and the sole end and aim of which was to extend relief to suffering, in whomsoever felt, or in whatsoever shape it presented itself. Neither can it be said that her conduct was instigated by selfish ambition or the thirst of applause; for on that lonely island no eye beheld the deed save that of Him who sees amidst the darkness of the tempest as amidst the light of the noon-day sun. Her only incitement could have been those feelings which the poet describes as universally characteristic of her sex:—
>
> "Her's is warm pity's sacred glow—
> From all her stores she bears a part,
> And bids the stream of hope reflow
> That languished in the fainting heart."
>
> The situation of Grace Darling is a peculiar one for a young female, and one which, we suspect, very few of her sex would envy. Living on a lonely spot in the middle of the ocean, amidst the widest war of the elements—with the horrors of the tempest familiarised to her mind, and her constant lullaby the sound of the everlasting deep and the shriek of the wild sea gull—her only prospect that of the wide-spreading ocean with the distant sail on the horizon—she is thus removed far from the active scenes of life, and debarred, save at distant intervals, from any communication with her own sex, and from all those innocent enjoyments of society and companionship which, as a female, must be so dear to her. And these are circumstances which go a long way to enhance the admiration due to her generosity and heroism; for it is well known that the natural effect of solitude and seclusion is to deaden all the kindlier feelings of human nature; and of solitude amongst the most awful scenes of tempest and gloom, to imbue the breast with a portion of their own savage character. And yet amidst all these adverse circumstances do we find her evincing a depth of feeling, and a nobleness of soul, which we might look for in vain amongst many of those of either sex who are pampered in the lap of luxury, and surrounded with every blessing which wealth, ease, and unrestrained freedom can bestow.

They have romanticised my existence. They don't understand I have lived here since I was ten years old. They are right in saying though that I have the horrors of the tempest in my mind, I still see their faces, I doubt I will ever forget that awful scene, ever.

30th November 1838

These months has been the busiest of my life. The Duke very kindly arranged for subscriptions to be set up as a fund for me, I am now seen as a charity, someone to donate money to. Of course I appreciate the kindness and thoughtfulness the Duke has shown, but I just want all of this attention to die down. It is good that there are also funds set up for the sailors who attended from North Sunderland, including my brother, as they also risked their lives in those treacherous seas, and the Duke told me my brother Brookes was the first in the boat.

I have had many men visit me, some are looking for a wife, and some have proposed but I have had to turn them down. I am not ready to get married yet, I am still only 23 years of age, and too young to be with one man for the rest of my life, and anyway, Mother and Father need me, I am the last to live here with them and I don't think Father could do his job without me. And Mother needs help with the housework and other chores. Thomasin said I should keep my name as it is now a famous name, and Father agrees, so we shall have to see whether I do eventually feel like marrying. I do want to have children one day though. The Duke has offered to be my Guardian, and filter my mail, and prospective husbands. He agreed to do this after several people were trying to take advantage of me, and some of these stories had been written about in the press. I got a lot of mail about the circus proprietor Mr Batty. He had invited me to attend the circus, and had offered to donate the takings from the nights entertainment, and asked if I wanted to attend. I had originally agreed, I thought it only proper, since he was dedicating the takings to charity in my name. But the letters I received were scornful, and didn't think my visit to the circus was fit for a heroine. They said I should not go, and was staining my name by agreeing to go. Having discussed it with my Father and the Duke, we felt it right that I should not attend for fear of him parading me around the ring like one of his circus animals. The press reported it wrongly saying he was offering me money to travel with the circus across the country. I only agreed to one visit, so it is understandable some were dead set against the idea.

I have received many gifts including money. I have received some medals, a gold medal and two silver medals for my bravery. My father and I each received a gold medal from the Royal Humane Society, and I received silver medals from the Leith Humane Society and the Edinburgh Humane Society.

Picture of my Gold Medal from the Newspaper.

A portrait of me by John Reay.

Some good however has come out of this publicity. After a public meeting in Newcastle Upon Tyne, they say there is going to be new legislation increasing the safety at sea. But the newspapers are still writing about me frequently. It seems that every little detail is recorded about me.

> **GRACE DARLING.**
>
> It affords us pleasure to announce that subscriptions have been opened at Bamburgh, Alnwick, and the respective neighbourhoods under the auspices of Lord Crewe's trustees and the Duke of Northumberland, for the purpose of marking the general opinion of the heroic conduct of Grace Darling and her father on the occasion of the late melancholy shipwreck of the Forfarshire steamer at the Fern Islands, and also of the gallant intrepidity of the seven boatmen of North Sunderland, who put to sea on the same occasion at the great hazard of their lives. We trust these subscriptions will meet with the success they so richly merit, and that all classes of our countrymen will testify, by contributing even the smallest amount to the fund, that admiration of the intrepidity of these parties which is so universally felt. The Duke of Northumberland is taking deep interest in the subscriptions now in progress for rewarding these humane and deserving persons, and his Grace recommends the sums collected in the several ports where subscriptions have been commenced to be united in one fund, in order to have the money appropriated in a way most likely to be of permanent advantage to the parties. There is much prudence in the suggestion; for otherwise the rewards, if received by instalments, might in some cases be expended unthinkingly; whereas, if the disposal of the money be left to a few judicious individuals, acquainted with the feelings and wants of the parties themselves, there can be little doubt that it will be beneficially expended. It appears that subscriptions are in progress at Durham, Birmingham, Dundee, Glasgow, Edinburgh, and other places, and we are glad to learn that, in order to mark their sense of the heroic conduct of Miss Darling in the affair of the Forfarshire, the directors of the Glasgow Humane Society have sent her their honorary silver medal, bearing the following inscription:—" Presented by the directors of the Glasgow Humane Society to Miss Grace Horsley Darling, in admiration of her dauntless and heroic conduct in saving (along with her father) the lives of nine persons from the wreck of the Forfarshire steamer, 7th of Sept., 1838." Since the disastrous shipwreck of the Forfarshire numerous parties have visited the Fern Islands. A lady and gentleman, on a pleasure tour, lately called at the Longstone Island, to have an interview with Grace Darling, when the lady particularly requested a lock of her hair to preserve as a memorial of her magnanimous and heroic conduct, which had been the means of exalting her yet more highly in public estimation. Numerous visitors, more especially the ladies, have solicited the same token from Miss Darling, so that the fair sex are by no means envious of the distinguished eminence she has attained, and are the readiest to render homage to her exalted conduct. The danger of her perilous undertaking is placed beyond all possibility of doubt by the fact that the boat's crew from North Sunderland could not return to the shore for two days and two nights, in consequence of the tempestuous state of the sea, and were obliged to take refuge at the lighthouse till at last they were forced to leave for want of provisions, the supply having been exhausted by the persons saved from the wreck, and who could not be brought ashore till the Monday.—*Newcastle Journal.*

It seems news of me also funds the newspaper as they seem to carry a story about me almost every day. They have even started printing the letters I have written to individuals to thank them for their gifts.

Those letters were written in private, and were for their eyes only, but now every time I write a letter I shall have to think of a much wider audience.

I have attached a cutting here of the newspaper article about my letter to the Glasgow Humane Society for their silver medal. I have received in total four medals now.

MISS GRACE H. DARLING.—Nothing can equal the present popularity of this young lady, save and except the conduct which has merited it. Not only are subscriptions in progress in all large towns to make her a pecuniary remuneration, and Societies in all parts of the kingdom forwarding their emblems of merit, but private individuals seem to emulate who are to be most prominent in acknowledging her services. Last week a gentleman passed through this town (Berwick) on his return to Edinburgh, from a visit to the outer Fern, having gone there to gratify himself with a sight of the heroine, when he carried with him a lock of her hair, for which he presented the original possessor with a sovereign. We lately intimated, that the Glasgow Humane Society had forwarded to Grace Darling their honorary silver medal. The following is her reply to the letter which accompanied the medal:—

Longstone Lighthouse,
5th Oct. 1838.

SIR,—I own the receipt of yours of the 20th ultimo, which has been delivered to me by Robert Smeddle, Esq. of Bambro' Castle, and in reply most respectfully beg leave to thank you as President, also the Committee and the members individually, for the kind present which they have thought proper to confer upon me. Be assured, that I lament most sincerely the awful loss of human life caused by the loss of the Forfarshire. It affords me great pleasure to think my humble endeavours, assisted by Divine Providence, have been instrumental in saving the lives of nine persons: but oh! how much my heart yearns within me to think how many valuable lives have been lost to their mourning friends and to society at large on this most melancholy occasion. I sincerely thank you on behalf of my dear father, and beg leave most respectfully to say, that the medal which your noble institution has been pleased to confer upon me shall be considered a valuable relict so long as it shall please Almighty God to spare me in this world.

I have the honour to remain, Sir,
Your very humble servant,
GRACE HORSLEY DARLING.

I feel as if I am constantly under scrutiny with a magnifying glass. Everything I do or say or write will be printed for the world to see. If I trusted the journalists it would not be as worrying, I have read a lot of nonsense written about me. Sometimes companies make up stories to help them sell their goods. It's astonishing the lies that are told, I hope the British public take most they say with a pinch of salt.

It has even been reported that I am my father's favourite child. So you can imagine the distress and jealousy this has caused in my family. Father loves us all the same; I just hope they don't believe everything that is written in the press. All of this idol worship has gone too far. They are writing poems about me, writing books about me, writing songs about me and writing plays about the rescue. I get requests for my hair with almost every letter. If I give away any more hair surely I will be bald. They put the hair in lockets and pendants. Some of them sell it. My hair is now valuable. I try to reply to the letters, but it is becoming more and more difficult as there are so many.

I hope next year will be calmer. I pray for all of this mayhem to calm down.

December 26th 1838

It seems I can't escape from the wreck. I was happy we were all together again as a family this Christmas, but it seems all they want to talk about is the wreck, and the newspaper stories.

I am worried my brothers and sisters are jealous of all the attention I am receiving. The Duke of Northumberland gave us a huge box full of presents for Christmas. My father got a waterproof coat, I cannot believe fabric can be waterproof, he tried pouring water on it, and it just slid right off it. It means he can now go out in the rain without getting wet, but he says he won't wear it. Mother got a silver teapot, and a waterproof cloak. I got a beautiful silver watch, with keys to wind it. I also got a waterproof cloak and some beautiful books, a prayer book, and the notes on the Bible.

The Duke is a very caring and thoughtful man, and I shall write to him to thank him for these wonderful gifts today. He has helped me enormously with my mail, and he is also looking after my trust fund, so far hundreds of pounds have been donated. I owe him much.

1st December 1839

It has been a little quieter this year than last year, thanks be to God. Although the newspapers are still writing about me, and visitors still come to the lighthouse, hoping I will entertain them. I usually find time to say hello to them, then Father rescues me, and takes them on a tour of the lantern. The Duke wrote to me last month asking if I had heard from the survivors from the wreck. I told him I hadn't heard anything. I do hope they are all well. He has been sorting out the money owed to me through the fund. He says they have collected around £725 for me, and he thinks he should pay me something now to use as I wish, and the rest he says would be better invested, and I shall be paid the interest at regular intervals. It all seems like a perfectly good idea to me. If anything happens to me the money shall go to my parents. It is a lot of money, more than my father could earn in ten years.

I am looking forward to Christmas; I am looking forward to seeing George and his new wife and his little baby Thomasin, and William's new baby William.

As well as tending to the lighthouse, writing thank you letters and such like, I have also been knitting baby clothes. I hardly ever have a minute to spare. This diary is sure to suffer for that too.

30th June 1942

I woke up during the night soaked in sweat. It is the fifth night in a row this has happened. I have a fever, but the medicine I have been given is doing little to bring it down or ease my cough. My chest is painful when I cough, but I can't tell my family as they would worry too much. It started about a month ago; I must have picked it up from one of the visitors. There was a man here in April who was coughing a lot, and mother got ill soon after, and now I, but I may have caught it when I was ashore in April. Father though has not ailed. The cough makes me weak, I find it takes me longer to row to Brownsman, as I get breathless with the exertion, and when the cold wind catches my breath it makes me cough sometimes that I can't stop. Brookes lives next to us now on the Island, Trinity built him a house and he is now assistant Lighthouse keeper so frees me some time, but I still help look after the light from time to time. His son little William keeps us entertained, but he is a handful, and is now into everything. I try not to cough if he is near, or my family are near, in case they catch it, so I tend to do a lot of my coughing in my room.

1st September 1942

I have had a wonderful day out today with my cousins. I rode a pony for five miles. The others were in the cart. I think they sent me out on my own on the pony so they didn't spend time near me. I think they are fearful of catching this cough. It worries me in case others catch it. I try to always cough into a handkerchief. But sometimes I cough up blood and they saw, and I think it really worried them. They said they had friends who had the disease who died, they are worried about me, but I feel much better today, I think I am over the worst. It was a beautiful day. I hardly coughed today. I think the warm country air helped. It was lovely just to be out and about.

We have received an invitation to visit our cousins in a few weeks in Alnwick. Thomasin and I are so looking forward to it.

18th October 1942

My health seems to have worsened. When I was staying with my cousins, they contacted my father about my health, and he came to see me in Alnwick. He spoke with the Duke, and he arranged for his physician, Dr Barnfather to visit me. He suggested I was moved to more pleasant airy surroundings, and I was put up in a house in Prudhoe Street, which was a very beautiful house. However, my father wanted me back in Bamburgh, he was worried about all of the attention I was getting, when people found out I was in Alnwick, they kept knocking on the door. Thomasin too thought it better I was with her in Bamburgh and so I agreed to go with them.

I have given Thomasin a list of things to get for me from Longstone. I would like to give my family some gifts as a thank you to them. I have too many gifts given to me, I want to give them something to remember me if the time comes. I am feeling weaker; this cough is making me so breathless.

I am reading St John's Gospel from the New Testament book the Duke gave me. St Cuthbert read from the same Gospel before his death, and I fear my time to be with the Lord is near. I am still only 26 years old so I hope God spares my life, but I am fearful I won't be here for my 27th birthday next month.

I give thanks to the Lord for my life and my family, to the Duke of Northumberland and all who have supported me and my family. I pray they do not mourn for me and give praise to the Lord for the memories we have shared together. In his Holy name. Amen.

> Grace Darling
> 24th November 1815 - 20th Octobe4 1842
> RIP

Grace Darling died in her father's arms on October 20th 1842.

Grace Darling is buried in St Aidan's Churchyard. Opposite the house where she was born.

Nearby is the Grace Darling Memorial.

In Bamburgh the town where she was born and where she died, is the Grace Darling Museum.

More Books by Sarah Lee

If you have enjoyed this work of fiction about the life of Grace Darling you may enjoy other books by the author Sarah Lee.

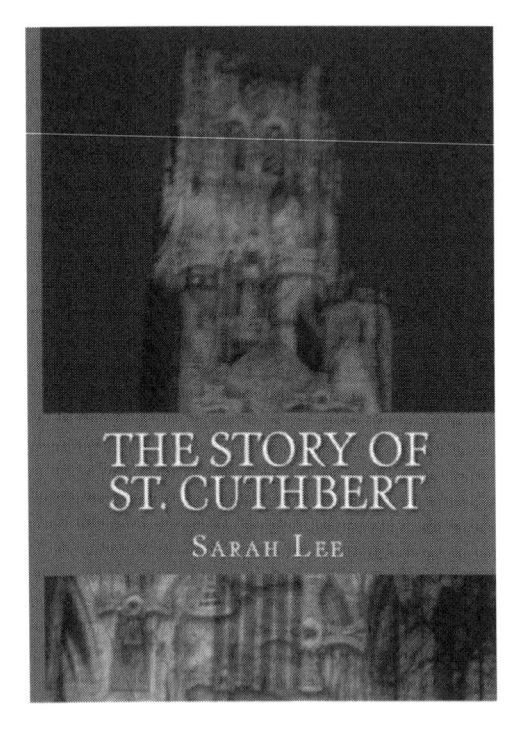

A story book about the life of St Cuthbert. He died on the Island of Inner Farne, not far from Longstone.

A travel guide on North East England, ideal if you are wanting to visit the Farne Islands. Advice on boat trips to the Farne Islands included.

Printed in Great Britain
by Amazon